PLAY BALL!

Jorge Posada

with Robert Burleigh

Illustrated by Raúl Colón

A Paula Wiseman Book
Simon & Schuster Books for Young Readers
New York London Toronto Sydney

To my wife, Laura, and my children, Jorge and Paulina; to my dad for introducing me to the game of baseball; and finally to my mom for always being there for me.—J. P.

To Paula Wiseman, with many thanks—R. B.

In memory of Lauren—R. C.

ACKNOWLEDGMENTS
With special thanks to Laura Posada. In addition, the author and publisher gratefully acknowledge the help of Edgar Andino and Mark Lepselter.

SIMON & SCHUSTER BOOKS FOR YOUNG READERS
An imprint of Simon & Schuster Children's Publishing Division
1230 Avenue of the Americas, New York, New York 10020
Text copyright © 2006 by Jorge Posada
Illustrations copyright © 2006 by Raúl Colón
All rights reserved, including the right of reproduction in whole or in part in any form.
SIMON & SCHUSTER BOOKS FOR YOUNG READERS is a trademark of Simon & Schuster, Inc.
Book design by Einav Aviram
The text for this book is set in Antiqua.
The illustrations for this book are rendered in watercolor, colored pencils, and litho pencils.
Manufactured in the United States of America
10 9 8 7 6 5 4 3 2 1
Library of Congress Cataloging-in-Publication Data
Posada, Jorge.
Play ball! / Jorge Posada with Robert Burleigh ; illustrated by Raúl Colón.
p. cm.
"A Paula Wiseman Book."
Summary: Presents a story of right-handed Jorge Posada being coached by his father to bat left-handed, and how it leads to the major leagues.
ISBN-13: 978-1-4169-0687-2
ISBN-10: 1-4169-0687-8
1. Posada, Jorge—Juvenile fiction. [1. Posada, Jorge—Fiction. 2. Baseball—Fiction. 3. Fathers and sons—Fiction.] I. Burleigh, Robert. II. Colón, Raúl, ill. III. Title.
PZ7.P838165Pla 2006
[E]—dc22
2005011767

I can't."

"Yes, you can."

"No, I can't."

"Yes. Get ready."

Jorge crouched in the batter's box. Everything felt strange. He was batting *left-handed* for the first time. He squinted toward the pitcher's mound, where his father waited. His father lobbed the ball. Jorge lunged awkwardly and missed—again.

The ball bounced to the backstop and rolled alongside four other balls that Jorge had swung at and missed.

This is impossible!

"I can't do it, Papa," the boy called. "I can't."

"Yes, you can."

His father trotted down from the mound to home plate. He stood behind Jorge and gently curled his arms around his son. "Hold the bat this way," he said, moving Jorge's hands slightly. "And bend your knees a bit more."

Jorge's father stepped back. Jorge swung at the empty air. "It feels weird," he complained. "I'm good batting right-handed. Do I have to—"

"*Good* isn't *best*," his father broke in, at the same time picking up the baseballs and heading back to the mound.

It was early Saturday morning and Jorge and his father were the only ones on the field. Jorge's father threw and again Jorge swung and missed. On the next pitch Jorge got a small piece of the ball. It flew upward, clanged against the cross-wired top of the batting cage, and landed in the dust with a dull plop.

"See?" his father called. "You're getting the idea."

"It's not even in fair territory," Jorge grumbled. Then he leaned forward once more, tensed his body, and waited.

Splat. The hard rubber ball echoed against the concrete wall. It was Wednesday. After the long bus ride home from school, Jorge wanted to do one thing: play baseball.

Splat, splat. When Jorge tossed the ball high off the wall, he drifted back and caught it on the fly. When he rifled it lower, he darted left or right to scoop up the resulting grounder. Jorge liked the *pop* sound when the ball went into the glove's wide, deep pocket.

"Hey, Jorge."

Ernesto and Manuel walked into the vacant lot. The three friends were always together. Jorge's mother sometimes jokingly called them "The Three Musketeers."

"Watch this." Jorge snared a ground ball and underhanded it to Ernesto, who spun and flipped it to Manuel.

"*Qué pasa?* What's up?"

Jorge walked over to where his bat lay on the ground. "Here's what's up," he said. Jorge put the bat on his left shoulder. "My dad wants me to start batting left-handed *and* right," he said with a glum voice. "To become a switch-hitter."

Manuel gave Jorge a baffled look. "That doesn't make sense. You're already a good hitter—batting righty."

Ernesto broke in. "No. It does make sense. Batting left-handed makes it easier to hit a right-handed pitcher."

"I guess so," Manuel admitted. "Remember that big right-handed Roberto guy we played with last week in the park? When he pitched sidearm, I thought the ball was coming smack at my head. Whoa, scary!"

"But I didn't strike out," Jorge spoke up.

"Next worst thing," Manuel teased. "A couple of lame taps to the pitcher!"

The three boys were silent. Then Jorge grinned shyly and said, "Well, maybe I *should* practice a little—left-handed."

They played "pepper." Ernesto and Manuel fielded. Jorge batted. His swing felt smoother. Sometimes he even made contact and sent a bouncing ball to one of his friends.

Every chance he had, Jorge swung and swung. There were some dry bushes at the edge of the lawn in front of his house. Their tops came up to Jorge's waist. He crouched and swung again. He tried to just skim the tops of the bushes.

He swung slowly and evenly. Then he stepped forward and swung with all his might. He felt his wrists snap around cleanly. He spun on his heels. It felt good.

"More follow-through," Jorge's father called out from the porch, where, unknown to Jorge, he had been watching. Jorge swung again. His father went on: "Let's go to the park and I'll hit you some pop-ups."

"Yes!" Jorge shouted. He loved roaming the infield while his father lofted sky-high pop-ups that never seemed to want to come down. "Let's go right now—after I take ten more cuts."

His real name was Hector, but the team members called him "El Flaco," the skinny one. The team was Jorge's team, Casa Cuba. And tall, thin Hector was the coach.

Hector knew everything. He knew how a shortstop should charge a slow-rolling ground ball and fire it submarine-style to first base. He knew how an outfielder had to aim his throws at the cut-off man. Hey, Hector could even throw a mean curveball!

He knew something about Jorge, too. "You're good, little man," he liked to say. "And you can become very, very good if you want to."

Jorge grinned. He sometimes felt as if Hector were a second father to him. Today's practice was over, but Hector was still on the mound, pitching to Jorge.

If the pitcher was right-handed, like Hector, a left-handed batter had a split second longer to gauge his swing. A curveball bent in toward him, too, not at his ribs and then away. Jorge was beginning to understand what Hector meant when he said, "Baseball is a game of inches."

Hector threw again—a slow curve. Jorge timed his swing and drove a clean line drive into center field. "*Batazo!* You're doing it," Hector called out happily, pounding his fist into his mitt.

They walked together into the outfield to pick up the batted balls. Very soon Casa Cuba would play its archrival— Club Caparra, one of the top teams on the island. And Caparra's coach was Jorge's dad! Hector looked down and smiled at Jorge: "You ready for that, little man?"

Jorge swallowed hard. *Am I?* he wondered to himself.

A trip to New York City!

It was big. It was bigger than big. It was *grande*.

Jorge and his little sister, Michelle, had never seen so many people. "Hold my hand," their mother kept saying. And they did. A person could get lost here—easily.

They visited Chinatown. They went to the top of the Empire State Building. They strolled through Central Park. But the best was yet to come. . . .

On this day they took the subway. When they emerged from the underground, Jorge's father pointed: "Look. There it is."

Jorge blinked in the afternoon sunlight. Up ahead on the high concrete wall, big letters blared the name: YANKEE STADIUM.

Jorge caught his breath. Babe Ruth had played here! And Mickey Mantle, the greatest switch-hitter in baseball history!

They followed the crowd around a curved walkway that led inside, and took an escalator to the upper deck. From his seat overlooking the right-field foul line, Jorge looked down. His eyes traced a path from the smooth, dark infield to the ocean of green grass to the hanging roof trim and on up into the summer sky.

There was a little flower garden behind a part of the outfield wall. His dad passed Jorge a pair of binoculars. Small monuments were in the garden. It was all so real and unreal at the same time.

Jorge's father spoke softly. "Their names are all there: the Babe, Lou Gehrig, the others. Forever."

Jorge gazed at the monuments. He put the binoculars down. He paused. "Some day I'm going to play here," he announced excitedly. His mother and father smiled at each other. "He will, I know he will," Michelle blurted out.

Just then the Yankees broke from their dugout. Tall Dave Winfield jogged gracefully into right. Jorge raised the binoculars again and focused. He could even see clearly the number on the uniform of his favorite player!

At last the day of the big game arrived.

Play ball!

It was Casa Cuba versus Club Caparra. Lots of people were watching, which made Jorge try harder—and feel extra nervous, too.

Things weren't going well either.

Pitching for Caparra was—yes!—the same Roberto that Jorge had batted against in the park. Jorge batted right-handed then. Now it was left. But what did it matter?

First inning: strikeout on three pitches.

Third inning: a weak bouncer to first.

Fifth inning: another strikeout.

Eighth inning: and yet another!

Jorge was replaying in his mind his woeful day at the plate, when—in the top of the ninth—a simple ground ball went right through his legs. Zip! A base runner scored and Caparra crept ahead.

Jorge wished he could hide under the second-base bag. He stood there all alone, with the sun beating down, until the half-inning ended. He trotted in and slumped onto his team's bench. The game was as good as over.

But after two quick outs Casa Cuba's luck changed—slightly. First an error; then two bases on balls. Jorge picked up his bat and walked slowly toward the batter's box. He heard his teammates calling his name. He also heard the opposing catcher chattering at the pitcher: "Easy out, Roberto. Easy."

Jorge hesitated. He would bat right-handed this time! Enough of switch-hitting! It wasn't his idea! *This is impossible!*

Then he remembered. He walked to the left side. If it really was a game of inches, he would take his one-inch advantage. He crouched as Roberto fired a sidearm rocket. Jorge saw the ball coming. He swung. It was only a foul tip. And yet: It felt good.

"Yes, you can."

Roberto delivered again. Jorge swung. The bat whipped around in one complete arc as its fat part caught the ball perfectly. Jorge, already running, saw the ball zoom over the second baseman's head and higher still into the alley in right-center.

Go. . . .

He didn't need to slide into second base. But he did—for the sheer joy of it. He knew two runners had scored on his double. Casa Cuba had won, had won.

"*Batazo!*" "*Batazo!*"

Jorge stood up and turned to see teammates racing toward him. He looked for his father. His father wasn't running toward him, though. He was merely standing by the Caparra bench with his arms crossed over his chest. Then Jorge was lost in a swarm of happy, leaping bodies.

In the car on the long ride home, Jorge's father was quiet. Jorge's mother asked questions about the game. Jorge's sister piped up. "He's the best, he's the best—isn't he, Papa?"

Jorge's father broke into a smile. "Well," he said, reaching over and rubbing Jorge's head, "he's getting better and better. Yes."

Michelle went on: "Can we stop for a pizza? Can I choose the toppings? Please."

Their father chuckled. "Pizza? Okay. But Jorge gets to choose. Tonight," he went on, "it's two toppings. One for the right side— and one for the left!"